Mistress of Night

Tiffany Putenis

Cask & Castle Publishing

To those who had to do whatever it took to survive.
You are worthy. You are seen.
You are loved.

Contents

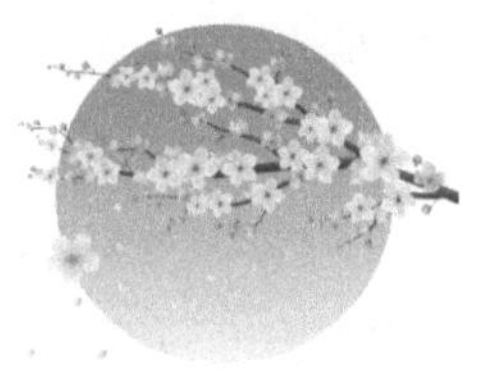

Chapter One

1740

Reisu Heiwa floated in the tepid water of the lake, unaware that the trajectory of her entire life was about to change. The waters in Lake Seishi, hidden deep in the heart of Tsuki Sōgen, were quiet, only disturbed by the gentle ripples of water coming off her body as she kept herself afloat. Birdsong filled the early spring air, the chirping providing a cheerful counterpoint to the meditative calm the water brought to her.

I wish I didn't have to sneak out to get this kind of peace, she thought. The weight of her parents' expectations bore down on her; she nearly sank deeper into the water as she thought of them. *Always the dutiful daughter, the perfect heir to the family legacy. Prophesied to become the Mistress of Night, whatever that means. Bearing the weight of everyone's expectations, hopes, and dreams. Destined for greatness, despite never longing for more than a moment's peace in the still waters of a hidden lake.* In the distance, leaves rustled as a flock of starlings took flight from their perches amongst the branches. The bright sunlight dimmed as clouds moved across the sky, distracting Reisu from her reverie; the angle of the sun alerted her to how long she had been floating, the skin of her fingers and toes now wrinkled from her extended soak in the lake.

She swam to the shore and climbed out of the water. She grabbed her towel from the tree limb and sent cherry blossom petals fluttering to the ground. Humming thoughtfully as she dried herself, Reisu twisted her damp hair back into a loose bun at the base of her skull, holding it in place with a hairpin shaped like a dove. Gooseflesh pebbled her skin as a sudden chill filled the air, ominous dark clouds springing from nothing to cover the sun. She hummed softly to herself as she rushed to finish dressing. Slipping on her sandals, she grabbed the age-worn linen towel and rushed from the lakeshore toward the packed-earth path leading back to her family's village.

"Miss?" A deep voice shouted as she strode purposefully toward home. "Please, miss. I just need a moment."

Reisu turned toward the voice, searching for the speaker. "Where—"

"Over here." The voice came from the shadows along the edge of the forest, feeble and scared. "Please help. I had a fall and landed over here, just off the road."

She rushed toward the forest's edge, mindful of her footing as she approached the sloping edge of the path. She saw the old man, his bald pate almost seeming to gleam despite the incoming storm. His leg was twisted beneath him, a silvery glint of bone protruding from his shin. Pain shone in his dark eyes, nearly black in the dimming light.

"Oh no," Reisu exclaimed as she hurried to his side. "Your leg. I'm not a healer, I'm afraid I can't..." She trailed off as he transformed before her eyes.

Shadows coalesced and twisted across his skin, peeling away the elderly visage to reveal a striking face. He possessed a chiseled jaw and eyes that glowed, colors swirling within them like the galaxies she had studied alongside her grandfather. He grew in height, his broad shoulders and arms stacked with muscles where the linen of his tunic stretched at its seams.

"I apologize for the ruse," he said, his voice deeper now, almost musical in its timbre. "I have been studying you for some time and knew that you would not approach me as I am now."

Reisu backed away, angling herself toward the path. "You've been studying me?" she asked, trying to keep him talking as she determined the best way to make her escape. "Whyever would you do that? I'm not particularly interesting." She took a step backward, angling herself toward the path.

"Tut tut," he said, throwing a solid barrier of shadow behind her. "You can't trick me, Reisu, though I know you are quite the clever girl. Now, don't you want to know who I am? I'm sure you know who I am."

"Not really. I want to go home. It's nearly time for tea." She flinched as he arched his eyebrow at her tone, years of training to be a bride and leader of her family suddenly at war with her desire to flee.

"I don't think you do," he said, taking a step closer to her. "Your heart is racing like a rabbit's."

"Let me go," she said, trying to regain the calmness she had felt at the lake. She shook her head, her hair sliding free from its pins. "I won't say anything to anyone; I won't mention this at all. Just let me go."

"Sweet little rabbit. You belong to me," he said. "I'll ask again. Do you know who I am?" Tendrils of shadow twisted from his form, pulsing as they absorbed the light around him.

"Dal'gon." She gasped. "The shadow demon."

He chuckled as he reached out with tendrils of shadow, threading them through her hair and pulling her head back to expose her neck. "The one and only," he whispered, stepping closer. His breath feathered across her ear as he leaned closer. "And I have been searching for you, Reisu Heiwa. Lone daughter of the Heiwa clan, heir to the family's legacy and the weight of their expectations, destined to become the night."

A rush of fear in her veins tightened her chest. "I don't know what you're—"

"Shh. Little Mistress of Night, guardian of the moon's light," Dal'gon said, nuzzling her neck. "Mmm, you smell so sweet—like innocence and cherry blossoms. You will soon understand, little rabbit. Come with me, and I will set you free. That's what you want, isn't it? To be free of the expectations that weigh on you?"

Reisu blanched at his astute assumptions, struggling in his grip as she realized he planned to take her. He pulled the shadows tighter in her hair, preventing her from moving, and yanked her head backward, ramming it into the shadowy barrier behind her. Her body went slack at the impact, unconscious from the trauma to her skull, and he lifted her into his arms as a portal opened behind him. He turned, shifting them forward, and moved into the pulsating shadows.

The denizens of the shadow realm bowed before Dal'gon as he cut a path through the crowd, carrying Reisu in his arms like a trophy. The creatures cheered and howled as he sauntered to his throne, laying her unconscious body on the black granite slab before it.

"The Mistress of Night now belongs to the shadow realm," Dal'gon announced as he turned to his disciples, his orotund voice filled with pride. The crowd of faces—his children and the lesser demons who populated his realm—let out a cheer at the announcement. He gestured to the side of the dais, waving one of the disciples forward.

"Master," Dalton said, appearing from the shadows at his side, "how can I be of assistance?"

"Ensure I am not interrupted," Dal'gon replied, bending to lift Reisu back into his arms. "I must complete the ritual so she cannot ascend."

Hidden within the crowd, Maddox watched as his father carried the delicate young woman through the gates of the keep. A crease formed between his brows as he studied her small frame and the petite features of her face. The tilt to the tip of her small nose caught his eye, making him wonder what she'd look like when she laughed. Though he didn't know why, he felt drawn to the girl in his father's arms.

Yours, a lilting voice whispered in his ear. *Claim her.*

‹‹●●●››

Consciousness was slow to return, the terror of being taken by Dal'gon holding her under. Pain ripped through her, the hook deep inside her chest pulling at her soul. The cold, clammy air of the seaside cave chilled her skin. She felt a pull inside her, as though something vital was being drained away without her consent. Eyelids fluttering, her head rolled back and forth on the stone slab as she tried to focus her eyes on something. Anything. Runes glowed black on the floor around the altar, creating a strange ambiance with the dueling scents of brimstone and candle wax filling the air. Despite the glow from the runes and the candle flames, darkness surrounded her, the shadowy depths covering her like a cloak of night.

Where the hell am I? she thought, struggling to stay alert in the dancing shadows. *What's happening?* She turned her head slightly, meeting his eyes.

"That's it," Dal'gon whispered as she struggled to keep her eyes focused. "Eyes on me, Reisu."

She stared at him, trying to focus on his face, trying to remember what happened, how she got here. Pain wracked her body, nearly dragging her back into the sweet protection of unconsciousness. "I—"

"Shush, little rabbit. Keep your eyes on me and I will make you into everything you are destined to be."

She shuddered as that hooking feeling pulled again and again, seeming to yank her soul free from her body. She floated, unmoored like she had been in the lake, the wisps of her soul coalescing into the shape of her mortal form. Her body lay on the slab before her, empty. *No. This isn't happening. No. Gods, please...* she thought as memories of her life drifted away.

Dal'gon smiled, a self-satisfied look on his face. "You are free."

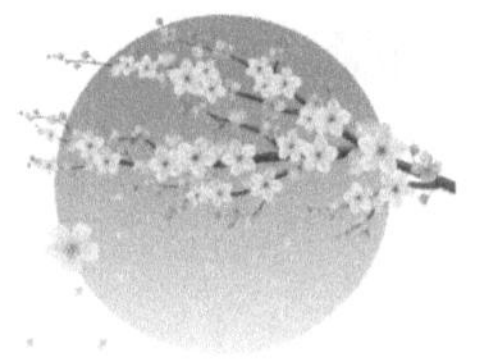

Chapter Two

1894

Reisu woke with a start, her wisps swirling tumultuously before solidifying into skin and bone. Beside her, Maddox snored softly, his face appearing almost innocent in sleep. The moon still reigned over the sky outside, casting the rooflines in her silvery light.

"Wake up," she said, shaking Maddox. "Get out of here before your father finds us like this."

He groaned, rolling onto his side and pulling her toward him. "Fuck him." He nuzzled his face into her abdomen, flicking his tongue on the sensitive skin just below her belly button. His lips curled into a satisfied smile as she shivered at the sensation.

Reisu squirmed in his grasp, reaching over to pinch the inside of his arm. "You know he'll kill you if he finds you in my bed. Get out of here!"

Maddox shrugged. "I really don't care anymore, Rei. Maybe the time has come for a change."

Reisu leaned in and pressed a kiss to his forehead. "Maybe it has. But the first battle shouldn't be in my bedroom." She shoved him playfully. "Go. Get out of here and back into your own bed."

She lounged back into her pillows and watched as he stood, reveling in the rippling muscles of his back as he pulled the shirt over his head.

"I'll see you later?" he asked as he tugged the laces on the front of his breeches closed.

"I'll be walking the halls of the brothel and keeping the clients in line."

"Then I'll come find you after I get back from whatever errands he has me running this evening."

Reisu tossed a kiss to Maddox as he walked to the secret passage hidden in the corner of her room. With a languid stretch, she rose from the bed and walked to her dressing room, her form shifting, her wisps flickering as the sun began to rise on the horizon. Watery morning light filled the room, glinting off of tin roofs in the dock district. Outside her open windows, people stirred to life. Sailors whistled jaunty tunes as they headed toward their ships, the calls of the gulls joining the melody.

She leaned against the frame of the window, looking out over the city. Her city for all these years, despite being thousands of miles from the only place she considered home. Envy filled her as she watched a woman chase after a small boy, barely four years old. His giggles echoed, sending a sharp pang of sadness through her heart. No matter how she longed for a family of her own, it could never happen. Dal'gon had ensured that when he ripped her soul from her body over a century ago. There would be no children for the Mistress of Night—her family line ended with her.

Can wraiths even die? she wondered as she watched the boy and his mother play. She shrugged away the thought and turned back to her wardrobe to dress for the day.

Despite the daylight and the bustle of activity beyond its doors, the brothel was quiet in the early morning hours. The girls slept in their private rooms on the top two floors of the building while Dal'gon rested in his chambers below ground. His favored sons would be slowly moving through the building at this point in the day. Maddox returned to his own chambers after their rendezvous; Dalton would be heading toward the gym. Kage was... Well, she didn't really know what Kage was up to. Nobody, other than Dal'gon, was ever aware of the missions he gave to his youngest son and disciple.

The overwhelming sense of ennui she'd experienced while watching the mother and son play in the street lingered despite her best attempts to dispel it. Rustling through the clothing in her wardrobe, dissatisfied with every option, she willed her wisps to solidify into an over-bust corset and skirt and bustle with sparkling silver skirt lifts. They swirled around her, the delicate gray of mountain mist, shimmering slightly in the sunlight from her windows.

"That works," she said as she glimpsed herself in the gilt-framed mirror that leaned against the dressing room wall. She wiped away a tear that still lingered on her cheek, despite her best efforts to brush away the sadness she felt and swept out of the dressing room. Grabbing the small ledger from her nightstand, she headed down to her small office near the brothel's foyer to watch the comings and goings of the clientele.

An hour and a half later, stooped over the largest of the ledgers upon her desk, Reisu rolled her head from side to side, desperate to stretch the aching muscles of her neck. Her head ached from the endless columns of numbers that lined page after page of the book, tracking each transaction that occurred within the brothel's walls over the past fortnight. This was the part of the job she hated the most: reviewing the veritable who's who of sexual deviancy that went on, and ensuring that all of the patrons were paid up on their accounts. She had never been a fan of politics or blackmail, but she knew of many wealthy men and women within Ship's Haven who would sell their souls for access to the black leatherbound book sitting before her on her desk.

Reisu found her personal ledger far more interesting; each entry detailed the comings and goings of Dal'gon and his disciples, tracking their movements and assignments. She flickered between her human appearance and her natural wispy form for a moment as she considered the latest entry, inked the night before.

July 23, 1894 - Maddox appears just after 10pm, blood flowing freely from a cut above his eyebrow.

"I wonder what he was up to," she murmured to the ledger before her.

"What who was up to?" a voice asked from the doorway. "Surely you'll have the answers inside your big book of secrets."

"Kage," Reisu said coolly. "How can I be of service to you this morning?"

"Oh, none of the usual debauchery for me, I'm afraid. Father had me out late, hunting some sort of weapon." He flipped his hair back across his forehead, his eyes twinkling with mischief. "No rest for the wicked, I'm afraid. No fun, either."

Reisu hummed softly, nodding her head in agreement. "I'm sure you don't need my assistance finding your chambers?"

"Not at all," Kage said, a smirk twisting up the corners of his full lips. "But if you wanted to join me inside them..."

"I'm afraid I'm otherwise...claimed," Reisu said. "You know your father. He doesn't like to share his toys."

Kage chuckled at her words as he turned to leave. "Before I forget," he said. "Father wanted to have a word with you after you've finished balancing the books."

"Of course. Thank you for letting me know; I'll find him as soon as I'm done."

Kage nodded and headed toward the stairs to the left of her office. Reisu released a sigh of relief as his footsteps faded into the dense carpet of the second floor landing.

That was dangerous, she thought. *Thank goodness I didn't pontificate more on Maddox's whereabouts last night... It would never do for Kage to realize that I've been tracking their whereabouts and activities.* She flipped to the next page in the ledger, dipping her pen into the inkwell beside her as she read through the list of services rendered to a Marquis the night before.

"Oh, Lord Dacre, what a naughty boy you were last night," she said as she tallied the charges. "Three at once, all of them with whips? My, what your peers in the government would say if they knew..."

"Three at once?" Maddox's deep voice sounded from the hidden passageway at the back of the room. "Whips and all? Fascinating."

"Would you like to try that, darling? I'm sure I can arrange it for you. So many of the ladies here would be happy to oblige a man of your...stature." Reisu turned in her chair, grinning as she felt him ward the room against eavesdropping; the wards solidified around them, ensuring they couldn't be overheard. A tendril of shadow twisted through the room, gently closing the door to her office and turning the lock. "Are you ever going to tell me how you ended up with such a magnificent amount of blood on your face last night?"

"In good time, Mistress. Everything in good time." Maddox leaned over her, his large hands on either side of the ledger behind her.

She felt her heart stutter as she looked up at him. "Your father..."

"Is undoubtedly unconscious four stories below us right now, deep in his lair."

"Kage was just here a few minutes ago, telling me he wishes to speak with me."

"He still wouldn't dare come to the main levels of the brothel in daylight, and you know it. Too risky for someone of his... How did you say it? Stature?" Maddox grinned, leaning forward to nuzzle his nose in her hair.

"Maddox." She shivered as the tip of his nose touched the sensitive skin of her neck.

"Yes, dearest?"

"If you don't remove yourself from my presence, I'll show you exactly what I can do with one of those whips against a man of your stature."

He nipped his teeth against the shell of her ear, drawing a small gasp from her. "Find me tonight and I'll tell you what happened," he said, his voice husky with desire.

"Tell me what happened or you won't find yourself in my chambers again," she said, her eyes filled with promise and fury in equal measure. "Now get out of my sight. I have work to do."

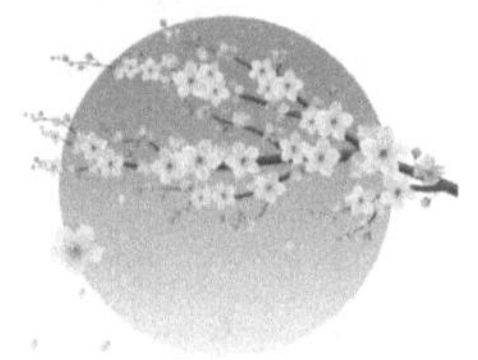

Chapter Three

Swirling shadows surrounded her as she descended the spiraling stairs leading down into Dal'gon's private apartments deep below the brothel. The large ledger held in one arm, she trailed her fingertips along the rich brocade wallpaper that lined the stairwell, counting each depression in the wall as she wandered in the darkness. The candles in their sconces would not stay lit this far below, no matter how often she relit them, and the maids refused to venture below the sub-basement anymore. Though she had no way of knowing for sure, Reisu had no doubt that Dal'gon had helped himself to a maid or two as they ventured down to light the sconces and sweep the dust from the stairs. The majority of them would never survive the psychic attack that occurred during the mating ceremony; she'd long since given up tracking how many maids went missing over the years. Only the strongest survived to bear Dal'gon's sons.

"Master," she called out. "You asked for me?"

"Enter." His voice echoed, seeming to fill the halls with the voices of all of his victims as he spoke.

Reisu took a deep breath, willing her wisps to become translucent, barely concealing her body beneath them. Her rosy nipples were peaked, their tips barely covered by the sheer fabric she'd conjured. Girding herself, she strode through the door, the very appearance of serenity. Dal'gon lay sprawled on the bed before her, uncaring of his nudity. Her eyes skimmed over his obsidian skin—he was objectively beautiful. The firelight glimmered across him, highlighting the planes and valleys of his abdomen and the angular cut of the muscles over his hips. The turgid length of his erection caught her eye, the tip glistening with a bead of moisture, as though he had been waiting for her. Despite her hatred of him, desire pooled low in her belly. She caught his smile as he scented her, the dampness between her thighs glistening in the candlelight as she approached.

"How can I be of service?" she asked, willing her voice into a subservient whisper.

Dal'gon patted the bed beside him. "Come. Sit beside me, Reisu."

She walked over to him, climbing into the bed to rest on her knees beside him. He lifted a hand and stroked a stray hair back from her cheek before grasping a handful of her hair in his fist and pulling her face to his. Their lips collided, sending her world spinning as lust and hatred warred within her. A gasp parted her lips and he slipped his tongue inside her mouth, stroking along hers before pulling it into his mouth.

He sucked on her tongue, sending shivers down her spine as her core turned molten. She felt herself leaning back onto the bed, her legs splayed wide for him as he continued to suck and nibble her tongue and lips. He dragged his lips from hers, grazing his teeth down the column of her throat before closing his mouth around one of her taut nipples. His nimble fingers found the other and she writhed beneath his attention, wetness pooling between her thighs at his ministrations.

"More," she gasped. "Please."

Dal'gon chuckled around her nipple, the vibrations sending shockwaves through her system.

"Please," she begged. "Inside me."

"No, little rabbit. Not yet."

A choked sob wrenched from her throat as he released her nipple and slid one of his hands up to grasp her throat. He squeezed gently, chuckling again as he felt the moisture growing between her thighs with the tip of his index finger. He slid the tip of it into her folds, stroking across the sensitive nub at the apex of her thighs, groaning as she bucked beneath him. Releasing her throat, he slid the rest of the way down her body and latched his mouth onto her clit, tracing the nub with his tongue before sucking hard. She bucked again and he pinned her thighs to the bed with his hands, thrusting his tongue inside her as she ground against him.

"Please, Master," she begged again.

"Shh," he whispered, blowing cool air against her as she writhed against him. A tendril of shadow wound up the size of the bed, wrapping around her wrists and pulling them high above her head as a ball of shadow found its way into her mouth, gagging her.

Reisu struggled against the restraints holding her hands above her head, her heart pounding in fear at the memory of being held, restrained and helpless, before he forced her transformation. She fought back against the orgasm that threatened to shatter through her with every thrust of his tongue, desperate not to give him her pleasure. He withdrew his tongue, licking up her entrance and flipping it against her clit as he slid two fingers inside her, curving them up to stroke the most sensitive part of her inner walls. Tears streamed down her face as her orgasm ripped through her, her body flickering in and out of wisp form as she struggled to control the magic that allowed her to feel corporeal sensations.

"Eyes on me, Reisu. Let me watch you as you come for me."

She opened her eyes, the gag of shadow holding her mouth open wide as she clenched around his fingers. He slowed his pace, watching as her head fell back. He released his hold on the shadows, the restraints and gag dissolving into nothingness, and he shifted her body so her head hung from the mattress.

"Open your mouth, Reisu."

She obediently opened her mouth wide, gagging as he thrust deep into her throat. She swallowed around him, giving herself a moment to adjust to his size as he filled her. He palmed her breasts, grasping them tight as he thrust rhythmically into her throat, driving himself toward completion. She grasped his balls in her hand and swallowed again, constricting the muscles around him, pushing him to the brink over and over again until she felt his muscles tighten. He pulled out and she felt the hot spurt of his orgasm coating the back of her throat as he withdrew slightly. She gently lapped at him with her tongue until he finished, swallowing every drop he gave her.

"Good girl," he said as he released her breasts from his grip, marked with bruises in the shape of his hands. His throat worked as he studied them, already hard and throbbing again at the sight of his markings on her skin. "On your stomach."

She sighed mentally as she rolled over. *It was too much to hope he'd be done with me after that, I guess,* she thought. He grasped her hips and rammed his cock deep inside her pussy. She clenched around him, already close from the feeling of him coming in her throat. As much as she despised him and his ownership of her body after the transformation, she lusted for each moment of his depraved touch. She had no choice.

"More," she begged as he pulled her hips into the air to meet each thrust.

He wrapped his hand around her throat and lifted her head back to allow him access to run his teeth along the sensitive skin behind her ear. Her moans spurred him on, and he used tendrils of shadow to work her clit as he slammed into her over and over with his hand around her throat.

"Come for me," he demanded as he pushed her further.

She writhed against him, filled with shame her desire for more as her pussy clenched around him, drenching him in the wet warmth of her release. He squeezed her throat tighter as her muscles fluttered, sending another gush of warmth from her as her orgasm intensified. Unable to hold herself up anymore, she went limp and he threw her body to the mattress, rapidly thrusting into her until his own orgasm overtook him.

Alone in her bathing chamber, Reisu slipped into the clawfoot tub. The heat of the water soothed her aching muscles as she washed the remnants of Dal'gon's passion from her skin. She scrubbed every inch of her skin with a loofah and cherry blossom scented soap, desperate to rid herself of the lingering memory of his touch.

"I hate him so much. Why do I still let him do that to me?" she pondered out loud, unable to look herself in the eye in the large mirror across from the tub. "What is wrong with me?"

She let herself slide deeper into the water, only her face floating above the surface. The gentle bobbing of the water around her reminded her of that day so many years before, when she floated in the gentle water of the hidden lake near her childhood home. Hidden by the copse of cherry blossom trees, she experienced what would be her last true moments of peace, completely unaware that her entire life would be upended that fateful afternoon. Though she had lived more than two lifetimes since that day, the loss of her innocence still ached like a fresh wound to her soul. She closed her eyes, the warmth of the water and the scent of cherry blossoms drawing her back into a long-forgotten memory.

"Mama," she yelled, running through the courtyard with the silken streamers chasing behind her. "Mama, look!"

She danced and twirled, the streamers flowing on the breeze behind her, following her movements and curving sinuously as she skipped along the path between the koi pond and the gently sloping lawn. Her mother laughed, a smile on her face at her daughter's antics.

"Reisu, though I love watching you dance and play, you must cease your foolishness and come attend me. It is time for your lessons."

"But Mama, I want to dance today."

"First you must learn to pour the tea and please your ancestors. The Sun God and the Lunar Goddess wait for no one, not even one with such promise as you, Reisu Heiwa. We can dance later, as the sun goes down over the orchard." Her mother sighed, gazing up at the cumulus clouds floating carelessly across the sky. "I will dance with you when that time comes."

Reisu sighed dramatically and gazed up at the sky, imitating her mother. "Yes, Mama." She followed her mother up the stairs into their home, where she would begin to learn the art of pouring tea.

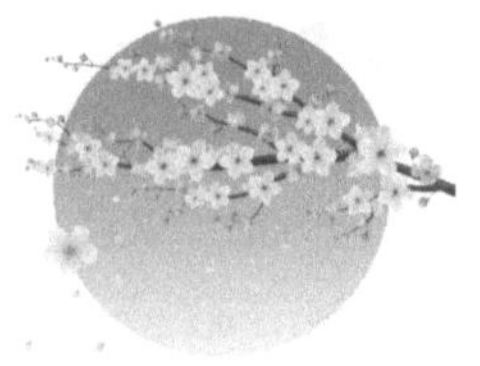

Chapter Four

Maddox walked into the office, slamming the double doors behind him. "What the fuck were you thinking?" he thundered, shadows emanating from his skin in waves.

Reisu's eyes flashed. Her wisps billowed around her, responding to his shadows. "Watch. Your. Mouth."

"I think we're beyond that, if you remember the things *my* mouth has done to you. But I was meaning your instructions to Kage."

"What instructions?" Her eyebrows drew together. "I haven't spoken to him in days."

"The disciples said..."

"Oh? Enlighten me."

"I was told you've sent Kage off in search of some weapon that could kill my father." His eyes searched her face. "Is it true?"

"Why would I do that? I didn't know there was such a weapon." Reisu sighed. "More likely that your father sent him to obtain it so he can eliminate the threat. They named me directly?"

"Yes."

"And you believed them?" She asked, incredulous. "Despite how well you know me and everything we've shared?"

"It seemed like... honestly, I didn't think. I just came here."

"Did they see you leave?"

Maddox's eyes widened. "Yes."

"This smacks of Dal'gon's machinations. He knows." She turned away from him, staring out the large windows that lined the back wall of her office, watching the sun stream through the remnants of the early morning rains.

"He couldn't know." Maddox grabbed her arm, turning her back to him. "Reisu, there's no way he knows."

"Then he suspects something. We must be careful, Maddox. You can't storm in here like this, asking as though you have a right to my time." She reached up, touching his cheek. "Nobody can know."

"Nobody will know. I will do what I must to protect you."

"As will I you," Reisu whispered. "As will I. Now, you must manufacture a reason to have stormed in here so suddenly. Shout at me by the doors. Throw them open and storm out."

Nodding, Maddox walked quietly toward the doors. "How dare you think you can tell me how to do the tasks Dal'gon has given me," he screamed. "You will pay for this, wench." He threw the doors open and turned back to her. "You will pay."

Reisu slumped into her desk chair, placing her head into her hands. One of the girls wandered by, looking into the room with confusion painted across her face. Reisu raised her head, letting the wisps flow around her, only her eyes visible. A growl left her throat. The girl's eyes grew wide and she turned quickly, scurrying away.

"Maybe now I'll be left alone for a while," she said under her breath, turning back to her ledgers. "Someone must keep this place running."

She carefully tallied the columns of numbers, tracking the girls' expenses and the incoming funds. Her eyes began to blur, her mind wandering, and the neat columns of numbers began to slant across the page.

Why would he send Kage out to hunt for a weapon? She thought. *Kage is the least experienced of his children. Unless he doesn't trust the others... they've all come into their power, so they're more of a threat to him.* She set down her pen, staring straight ahead.

"That's it," she mumbled. "He's trying to get the weapon before anyone else finds it so he can destroy it before they can use it against him." She grabbed a piece of stationary and jotted down a note, covering the ink with sanding powder to dry it quickly. Tucking it into an envelope, she hurried to the hidden slot in the corner of the room and slipped the letter through.

·‹‹❮●❯››·

The last vestiges of twilight painted the windows in shades of indigo and violet as the sun finished its descent behind the mountains to the west of Ship's Haven. Reisu locked the doors to her office and ascended the age-darkened mahogany stairs up to the second level of the brothel, pausing to peer through a discreet peephole hidden in the intricate damask wallpaper. With a small smirk, she watched the couple in the room.

A delicate brunette sat astride her gentleman caller, his hands fisted in her hair as he ravished her neck with his teeth and tongue. She writhed against him, grinding her hips into the hard length straining against the confines of his breeches. As a moan left her throat, the door burst open and another man, the patron paying for the scenario, stormed into the room.

Reisu grinned, pulling the small notebook from her satchel and jotting down a quick note. *Fascinating,* she thought. *He's chosen a cuckold scenario for the evening. That's different.* She pocketed the book and strode up the remainder of the stairs to the third floor, crossing to the nondescript door on the left. With two quiet raps on the door, she twisted the knob and slipped into the room, quickly closing the door behind her and twisting the lock.

"Finally," Maddox said from his chair beside the fire. "I thought you'd never get here. I've been waiting for hours."

"I sent you the note an hour ago," she said, arching a brow at him.

"It felt like hours. Why did you summon me? It must be something important."

Reisu sighed, seating herself on the chair across from him. "I had an epiphany about the mission Kage was sent on."

"Oh?" Maddox straightened, leaning forward and resting his elbows on his knees.

"Dal'gon is searching for the dagger so that he can remove it from play. If a weapon exists that can destroy him, he would need it out of commission so that he can maintain control of the shadow realm and disciples." She paused, staring into the flames. "I think, and maybe I'm just being paranoid… I think he's letting it look like I'm searching for it so that he can eliminate me."

"Why would he eliminate you? Who else would run this place?"

"If he suspects I'm pulling away from him because of you, I've become a liability. An alliance between us would shift some power away from him. He would no longer have complete control over both of us and it puts him at risk in the event someone plans a coup."

"Nobody is planning a coup, Reisu. The disciples are thoroughly under Dal'gon's control; they have no need to revolt."

"But what if *we* had a reason, Maddox?" She stared into his eyes intently. "What if he thought *we* were trying to eliminate him?"

He shook his head as he contemplated her words. "I don't think he would think that, Rei. There's never been any indication that we are aligned, let alone that we would be planning something."

"But what if we did plan something? I could finally be free. You could get out from his shadow and move toward a future of your own choosing." She slipped to the floor, moving toward him and placing her hands on his knees.

"We could be together for real, instead of sneaking into rooms and going out late at night, hunting for a fight," he said.

She nodded, looking away.

He cupped her chin, tilting her face up to get a better look at her expression. "You're serious."

"It dawned on me today," she said, sliding her hands slowly up his thighs. "His preoccupation with locating the dagger could be the distraction we need to move some key pieces into place. To start working toward futures of our own. Without him."

A low purr sounded from her as he slid his hand down the front of her throat, caressing her collarbones before dipping his fingers under the lace edge of her bodice. She slid her hands to the front of his breeches, popping the button free as he moved his hand deeper into her dress, grasping an already taut nipple between his thumb and forefinger. He worked her tender flesh slowly, rolling it between his fingers, as she slid his breeches further down his hips to free his cock. Finding him already hard, moisture beading at his tip, she leaned forward to lap at it, giggling when he fisted his free hand in her hair and pulled her face up to his. She moved to straddle him, hiking her skirts up around her hips as he deepened the kiss.

Maddox kneaded her breast, positioning the taut bud of her nipple between his fingers, and slid his tongue into her mouth, stroking along hers possessively. She arched into him, pressing her hips against the hard length of his erection and grinding against it. His moan of pleasure vibrated through her and she slid herself down onto him with aching slowness, savoring the stretch of her sensitive skin as he filled her. She gripped his shoulders with her hands, using them as leverage as she moved along his shaft, her muscles quivering from the contact. He gripped her hips in his hands, arching up into her and changing the angle slightly as his shadows trailed down her neck. She slid her hand down her body, her fingers finding where their bodies joined and feeling the slick wetness pooling at the base of his cock. Stroking her wetness over her clit, she circled and flicked herself in rhythm with his thrusts, her head thrown back as the orgasm ripped through her. She slumped forward against him, panting as he drove into her a final time, finding his own release.

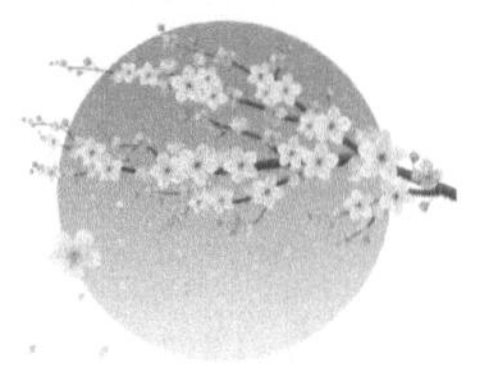

Chapter Five

Reisu willed her body into wisps, becoming a diaphanous cloud of near-iridescent smoke lingering near the sconces outside of Kage's chambers. The edges of her vision shimmered as she watched the corridor, wavering in and out as the hinges of his door creaked. Kage emerged from his rooms, dressed in all black with his hair artfully mussed. To anyone observing him, he would appear to be a rich young man out for a night of debauchery; indeed, he was just as likely to debauch himself while searching for the dagger as he was to stay focused on the task at hand.

I still can't believe Dal'gon chose him, of all the disciples, for a task he deemed so vital to their survival, she thought. *Though I suppose Kage's wild streak and focus on pursuing pleasure makes him ideal. He's never been the type to think up a plan on his own—he's definitely not the type to plan a coup.* Reisu watched as he slipped down the corridor, whistling a jaunty shanty as he took the stairs two at a time, then shifted herself forward. Careful to maintain enough distance that he wouldn't realize she was following him, she tracked him. They moved through the slums just beyond the merchants and inns that lined the narrow cobblestone streets of the dock district.

"Why ya hidin', little girl?" a voice shouted down the alley. "We just want to have a bit o' fun with ya."

Reisu watched as a young woman, clothed in a tattered bodice and skirts, pressed herself tighter against a wall behind a stack of crates. The raucous sound of sailors on shore leave echoed in the enclosed space, and Reisu watched as the woman twisted shadows around herself in much the same manner as Dal'gon and his disciples used them. Kage was at the mouth of the alley; she knew he had seen the shadows moving and his suspicions would be aroused, so she tucked herself closer into a stack of old wine barrels as he edged closer. The men chasing the young woman were completely focused on her, not noticing his approach.

"Oy, Franz, the little git is here somewhere," one of the men shouted, peering around crates and barrels. "She can't have disappeared."

A terrifying smile crossed Kage's face. Reisu watched as he opened the lid on a barrel that reeked of fish guts and decay, hiding something inside it and shifting the lid back into place. He tossed a rock toward the men to get their attention and draw them away from where the young woman hid. As he led them on a merry chase out the opposite end of the alley, the girl escaped, disappearing into the night without a backward glance.

Reisu waited amongst the wine barrels for a few moments longer, ensuring that Kage wouldn't return before creeping to the fish barrel and peeking inside. Atop a pile of fish guts and refuse lay a plain-worked dagger, its quillons engraved with the phases of the moon. Unthinking, she reached toward it, as though her hand moved of its own volition.

No, she thought. *He stashed it here with the intention of coming back for it. Don't touch it.* The dagger seemed to call out to her, something familiar in its plain silver blade and moon phases. It reminded her of her mother and a tapestry that hung on the wall of her ancestral home. The Heiwa home. She eased the lid back onto the barrel, careful to avoid notice, and shifted toward the lyceum and its storied library.

Home, she thought, her heart aching. *If anywhere has information on the dagger and drawings of the tapestries from my parents' home, it's the lyceum.*

A draft leaked through a broken window in the old storeroom within the scribes' quarters above the library, allowing Reisu access to the lyceum's archives. She aimed her wisps through the narrow opening and vaulted into the dimly lit room two floors above the main stacks. Not daring to light a candle, she relied on the ambient light from the moon as it shone through the narrow windows at the end of each row to find her way to the shelves of histories tucked away in the far left corner of the library. She searched for titles referencing the Heiwa clan or a dagger with moon phases carved into it on shelf after shelf, carefully placing each rejected book back in its exact location to avoid anyone noticing the books had been manipulated. She flipped through pages of a book titled *The Fall of Heiwa*, feeling an inexplicable pull toward a page in the center of the book. The ink-darkened page contained a sketch of the tapestry. She studied it closely, taking in the minute details—the moon phases, nearly identical to those engraved on the dagger; the carefully stitched characters invoking a prayer to the Lunar Goddess, Tsuki; the deep blue threads making up the sky, interwoven with shining silver stars.

"The matriarchal line of the Heiwa clan were ardent worshippers of Tsuki, believing their line to be directly descended from the Goddess herself," she read aloud in the barest breath of a whisper. "There are many mentions of Tsuki in reference to the Heiwa line, particularly the last matriarch of the dynasty. Tsuki... I wonder..." she trailed off as memory took over.

Her hair flowed freely down her back as she knelt before the altar. Above her on the wall, her mother's tapestry shone; the silver threads of the stars twinkled in the light of the candles scattered around the room to honor Tsuki, the Lunar Goddess. Reisu had long heard the stories of her mother's devotion to Tsuki and the many times she had prayed to the Goddess that she would become with child, the heir to the Heiwa line. Though her father had hoped for a male heir to continue their lineage, the Goddess herself was present at Reisu's birth, marking her the Mistress of Night, the prophesied savior who would return balance to the world in the Goddess's name.

Her mother had been overjoyed and believed that Tsuki had granted them a daughter to align with the prophecy, a girl who would bring honor to the Heiwa name. She spent many hours with Reisu, kneeling before the altar to Tsuki and prostrating herself in gratitude for the blessing of her birth. Now, as Reisu teetered on the edge of adulthood, they prayed together, searching for guidance on her future.

The smell of incense—sage, lotus blossom, and comfrey—filled the room, smoke swirling from the smoldering tips of the cones scattered around the altar. Her knees ached from her stationary position on the ground, but she knew she would be scolded if she so much as twitched during the ritual offering.

"Tsuki, Goddess of the moon, patron of House Heiwa, we call to you that you may hear our prayer. Shine your light on Reisu's future so that she may bring honor to our family."

Reisu flinched slightly as her mother prayed aloud to her chosen Goddess; the implications of the prayer for her to bring honor to their family were not lost on her. She had never behaved the way she was expected to, and it had caused many difficult moments between them. She hoped that she would cease to be a disappointment to her mother one day. Closing her eyes, she pictured the moon phases carefully embroidered onto the tapestry. She meditated on the image, imagining each stitch.

"Reisu." A pleasant voice spoke, seeming to surround her. "Daughter of Heiwa, moon-blessed at birth. What an enigma you shall become."

Reisu opened her eyes, looking around the room. Beside her, her mother remained knelt in prayer, unaware of the words being spoken.

"Child, you will do great things. But you must understand that, no matter how far gone into the shadow, there
is always a bit of light that remains. Be wary of the forest
path, for your destiny can change in the blink of an eye."
A soft chuckle wrapped around Reisu as she opened her
mouth to question. "So many questions in your mind. Know
this, young one—you must take care or your light will be
lost among the darkest shadows. Remember that your light,
however it dims, will always remain. You must only shift
perspective to see it shine."

The moons on the tapestry seemed to glow as the voice
faded away.

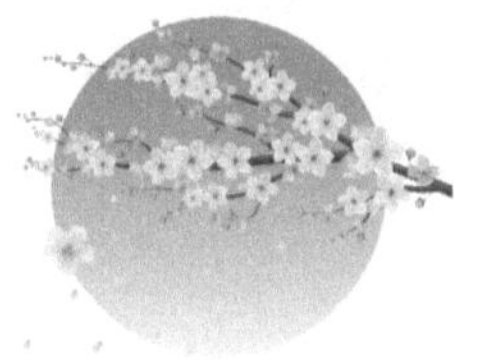

Chapter Six

Sweat dripped down Maddox's bare back as he shifted in the ring, dodging a punch from his opponent. The muscles in his arms bunched and flexed as he struck quickly, landing a strong punch to Dalton's abdomen and throwing him off balance before ducking behind him. Dalton swung wildly, desperate to land his right hook, but momentum knocked him to his ass. Maddox pressed a foot to his chest.

"Yield," he said, smirking.

"Never," Dalton said, grasping Maddox's ankle and yanking him down. They rolled together, fighting for leverage.

Maddox landed atop Dalton, straddling his chest and pinning his arms down with his knees. "Yield."

Dalton tapped the floor three times and Maddox stood, stepping away. Wiping the sweat from his face, he tossed the towel to one of the waiting attendants and grabbed his shirt from the ropes, pulling it over his head and adjusted the laces.

"Good match," Dalton said as he stood. "You didn't pull your punches this time."

"Maybe I decided to stop going easy on you," Maddox quipped.

"Or maybe you finally had proper...motivation."

A flicker of confusion flashed in Maddox's eyes and he shoved Dalton's shoulder. "Or maybe I was sick of hearing your smug bragging around the house and decided it was time to kick your ass."

A soft feminine laugh floated toward them, bringing a smile to Dalton's face. Maddox turned to see Reisu and one of the girls standing near the doorway of the gym, chatting as they watched them. She caught him staring at her and smiled.

"Maddox, a word?" Reisu said. "We have a situation with one of the gentlemen that requires your particular skill set."

Maddox waved to Dalton and walked away, heading to the stairs that led to the main floor of the brothel. Reisu trailed after him, her skirts swishing in time with his steps.

A small crease was between her eyebrows, a telltale sign of her concern as they walked toward her office. A rangy gentleman waited in a chair beside her desk, held in place by the bodyguards that worked the door to the brothel during operating hours. Blood trailed from his nose, one of his lips cut and swollen.

"Marcus, Nathaniel. What do we have here?" Maddox said, not bothering to hide his disdain for the patron seated before him.

"Hims thought he could rough up Belinda, sir," the taller of the two men said, squeezing his fingers into the gentleman's shoulder. "She got a real nice shiner, she does, and a bloody lip."

"We don't let gents do that to our girls," the other man added, his eyes glittering in anger. "Ain't nobody hurt our girls. We gave 'im the same as 'e gave 'er."

"Madame," Maddox said, turning to address Reisu, "how would you like me to deal with him?"

Reisu smiled. "However you wish. Just don't bloody my office too much. Come find me once you're done. And Maddox? Make sure you clean up your mess." She strode out of her office to the sound of knuckles impacting bone in a rhythmic symphony.

⋅‹‹●●›·

The maid brought up the final bucket of water, filling the massive copper tub to capacity. With a nod to Reisu, she exited the room, closing the door behind her.

"Finally," Reisu said as she slipped the dressing gown from her body and stepped into the tub. Her wisps danced along the edge of her form as the hot water contacted them; she slid deeper into the water, allowing it to engulf her.

Thoughts of the dagger and the moon phases filled her brain as she turned over the events of the past few days in her mind. *I wonder if the dagger and Tsuki are connected. It would make sense that one made of moonlight would have what is needed to defeat one crafted from shadows. Though I always assumed it was the angels that Dal'gon feared...*

A soft knock at the door jarred her back to the present.

"Alicia, I promise you I'm quite capable off..." she trailed off as Maddox slipped into the room. Blood caked his knuckles, deep bruises forming along the ridges of his fists. "Maddox."

"You did say to come find you," he said softly. "Though I didn't anticipate you being so charmingly displayed when I came in."

The water lapped against the delicate skin in the valley of her breasts as she moved within the tub. "I thought I'd have more time, to be honest. You usually take your time with such matters."

"I had other, more pressing matters to attend to," Maddox quipped as he pulled his shirt over his head and tossed it aside. He undid the button at his waist and slid his pants down his hips before stepping into the tub with her. A hiss left his throat as he sank into the water, bringing it dangerously close to overflowing the tub.

"Interrupting my bath, it would seem."

"And finding out what was so desperately important that you would manufacture a reason to see me this afternoon."

Reisu looked down at the water, swirling with steam and bubbles along its surface. Maddox grasped her chin between his thumb and forefinger, lifting her face so she would meet his eyes. Her caramel-brown eyes blazed with emotion he couldn't quite place.

"The girl wasn't nearly so brutalized that he required my attention," he said. "Though I agree that it is sometimes necessary to make our point to ensure future compliance with the rules. What did you discover?"

"The dagger," she said. "I followed Kage—he located it, but he stashed it in a barrel of fish guts in an alley so he could run off to save some chit who was being followed."

"How unlike him," Maddox said, stroking his hand across her cheek and down her neck. His fingers rested near her collarbone, gently tracing small circles on the delicate skin there. "He ran off without finalizing his mission? I would never have thought he'd have the balls."

"Regardless of whether or not he completed the mission and brought that dagger to your father, he recovered it. I saw it, after he ran off. I was careful not to disturb anything. I think it might..." she trailed off, emotion flickering across her face before she could hide it away. She leaned into his hand, just slightly, as his fingers continued their gentle massage.

"It might..."

"The engraving tickled my memory, so I did some research. My mother worshiped Tsuki, the Lunar Goddess. The same pattern as the engraving was embroidered on the tapestry that hung in our family shrine."

"The Lunar Goddess... it would make sense that a being of light could defeat one of shadow," Maddox said.

"Yes, I was contemplating that when you interrupted my bath," she teased, splashing water toward him. "I think the dagger and Tsuki are connected in some way. And they might connect to the Mistress of Night prophecy."

"Mistress of Night... That prophecy was about you. Or so they thought. When Dal'gon turned you, didn't that negate the whole thing?"

"I don't know," she said. "It had been at least a hundred years since I thought about it. But when I was in the lyceum—"

"You went to the lyceum? How did you manage to get in?"

"Don't ask. I did some research after I saw the dagger. It triggered a memory of my past."

Maddox stared at her. "You've never said anything about your past before," he said.

"I haven't thought about it in decades," she said. "It hurt too much, at first, then it just became a habit not to remember my parents and who I was supposed to be. But when I remembered the tapestry and started researching... Did you know everyone assumed I'd been drowned? That's what's written of me in the histories. That I drowned in a lake I wasn't supposed to be at while disobeying my parents."

"Reality was quite different."

"I didn't choose to come here, to become a monster," Reisu said, her eyes flashing. "I did not choose this life."

"I know, I understand," Maddox said, sliding closer to her. "I know you didn't choose this." He stroked his hands up and down her back.

She leaned her forehead against his shoulder. "I would give anything to go back to them," she whispered.

"I know."

"Anyway, the etching on the dagger is identical to the one that was embroidered in the tapestry. I found a picture of it in one of the histories written about my family."

"Fascinating," Maddox said, the whisper of his breath against her neck. He edged his mouth closer to her skin and scraped his teeth lightly along the sensitive skin behind her ear. "You know what else I find fascinating?"

"Mmm," she said.

"Mmm?"

Reisu tilted her head to the side, giving him better access as he nibbled his way down her neck. They shifted, her legs straddling his as he scooted her body closer, his hard length teasing her entrance. Water spilled over the edge of the tub, exposing her breasts to the cool air. Her nipples pebbled from Maddox's ministrations and the chill, and she shifted her hips forward, grinding against his length as he continued to nip and suck at the delicate skin of at the crux of her shoulder. A low groan escaped his throat as she rubbed against him. He slid his hand along her abdomen, tracing small circles on her skin with the tips of his fingers before dipping his hand between her legs. She arched against his hand, craving the tension building within her.

He leaned his forehead against hers, stilling his hand for a moment. "Why do you do the things you do?" he asked as their breath mingled between them. "Why do the smallest things you do set me on fire?"

Confusion furrowed Reisu's brow. "I don't understand," she said softly, staring into his eyes.

He captured her lips with his in answer, his tongue sliding along the seam of her lips before delving into the warmth of her mouth to tangle with hers. She gasped as he slid his cock against her entrance before pushing forward into her, her muscles stretching around him as she adjusted to his girth. He dragged his teeth down her neck again, making her clench as pleasure coursed through her. She rocked her hips toward him, taking him deeper and drawing a groan from his throat.

They moved together as he ran his hand through her hair, gripping it to angle her head so he could nibble and lick the sensitive spot behind her ear. She released a breathy moan, gripping his shoulders harder as he thrust deeper into her; she reached a hand between them and stroked the swollen nub of her clit in time with his thrusts, pushing herself closer and closer to the brink. He felt her muscles begin to flutter around him, her heart pounding against his chest, and shifted her slightly backward, changing the angle to stroke the sensitive spot inside her.

Reisu screamed, her breath catching in her throat as waves of pleasure threatened to drown her. "Maddox," she said. She chanted his name like a prayer as he spilled into her.

Maddox kissed her gently, cupping her face in his hands. "You are exceptional."

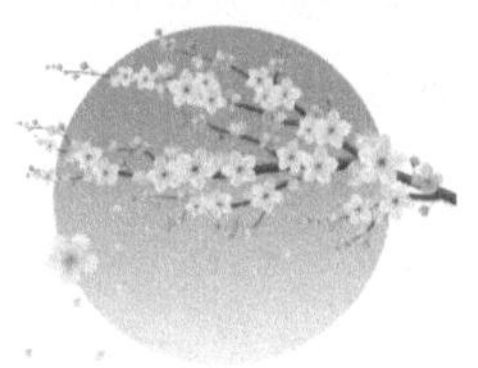

Chapter Seven

Reisu woke with the dawn, her mind unable to rest as she contemplated the meaning of the markings on the dagger and her mother's worship of the Lunar Goddess. She shifted into wisps, moving her body through the hallways of the brothel by lingering in the smoke of the candles and cigars left burning. Though gas lamps were present in the majority of the halls, heavy brass candelabras stood interspersed between the lamps to provide additional light for the patrons as they roamed the halls.

Thank gods for my foresight at leaving these candles lit last night, she thought. She snuffed the candles out as she moved down the hallway, shifting from smoke cloud to smoke cloud toward her target. *So much easier this way.*

Up two levels from her own rooms was Dal'gon's private study, the only room in the brothel he visited outside of his own chambers below. Down the hall from the disciples' quarters, it allowed him to be close to his sons to monitor their progress on their missions, as well as giving him a separate area away from his private rooms to discipline them when needed. She knew Kage must have retrieved the dagger; Dal'gon had been locked in his study for the bulk of the previous evening, risking being seen by the patrons, despite everyone being within their chambers and it being a quiet night within the brothel. If the dagger was anywhere within the walls of the building, it would be in his study, locked in the safe far from where he slept.

Reisu slipped through the gaps surrounding the door, hiding in the shadows that darkened the corners of the room. Dal'gon had left the study; she couldn't sense his presence in the room, and the shadows were still. The curtains were open, letting the watery early morning light into the room, lingering raindrops from the early morning storm dipping down the glass. The dim light revealed the ornate desk at the center of the room, papers with scrawls of ink in his distinct handwriting scattered across its surface. Shelves lined three walls of the room, filled with books and sculptures. But one shelf, she knew, was a facade for Dal'gon's safe. She shifted her wisps into her corporeal form, opening the narrow hidden drawer beneath the surface of the desk and slipping the key from its confines. She pulled the first, third, and seventh book forward, tilting them onto their spines, and released the facade, revealing the safe.

Opening the lock, she pulled the dagger from the safe, inspecting the delicate engraving on the blade. The whorls and loops carved into the bright metal surface revealed an elegant depiction of the night sky. The design called for her touch. She carefully traced the pattern with her fingertips, falling into the memory as easily as breathing.

"Reisu, pay attention," her mother said, tapping the parchment on the table between them. "This is very important."

"I understand, Mama." Reisu focused more intently on the drawing. "This symbol here," she said. "It is the moon, is it not?"

"You are close, Reisu. Very close. It is the symbol for Tsuki's chosen. It is said that Tsuki will choose her successor, the one who will become the Mistress of Night and rule the skies upon Tsuki's ascension to the final resting place of the gods."

"But gods do not die," Reisu said, a tiny furrow forming between her delicate eyebrows.

"Die? No, my dear, they do not die. They ascend and rest, allowing their chosen to rule in their place. You, daughter, were touched by Tsuki at birth." She tapped the small birthmark on Reisu's shoulder, the crescent identical to the symbol on the parchment before them.

"Yes, Mama, but what does that mean?"

"It means you are destined for something great, Reisu. Only the most pure of heart can be touched by the gods at birth; they are chosen for something more, though it is not known for many years what purpose they will serve. Your father and I believe that she has marked you as her chosen one, the future Mistress of Night. There is no record of anyone ever receiving her mark upon their birth. I know you chafe under the rules that we have given you as you come of age—"

"The pointless rules, you mean, Mama? The ones that prevent me from having friends, from swimming in the hidden lake, from walking alone?"

"They are not pointless, Reisu Heiwa. They are to protect you from those who would steal you, prevent you from taking your rightful place."

Reisu frowned. "What use is life if I'm not allowed to live it? I just want to live, Mama."

"And live you will, my child, when you ascend."

Reisu narrowed her eyes. "And until then I am to be a captive within my own home."

"Never a captive, my love. Merely a protected treasure, the future of our house and the chosen of our Goddess." Her mother reached out to touch Reisu's cheek, but she pulled away. "We want nothing more than to keep you safe from those who could hurt you or put your purity at risk."

"I see," Reisu said, resigned. "What else are we studying today?"

Reisu blinked as the memory faded, her fingertips still tracing the whorls and loops making up the pattern on the dagger. Her thoughts drifted back to her conversation with her mother, her desperate conviction that Reisu would be destined for something greater. A creak on the wood floor outside the room startled her, dragging her from her thoughts. She returned the dagger carefully, securing the safe and returning the key before shifting into wisps and disappearing into the haze of smoke lingering in the corners of the room.

She hastened to return to her own chambers, slipping through the passageways in shadows and smoke. The memory she recalled weighed heavily on her mind as she contemplated the meaning of her mother's determination and devotion to Tsuki and the idea that Reisu had been chosen by the Goddess for some purpose. Even now, so many years later, she remained clueless as to what that purpose may have been. Despite the promise at her birth, Dal'gon had ensured that she could never reach her promised potential the day he hooked into her soul and yanked it free of its corporeal shell. She was no longer pure.

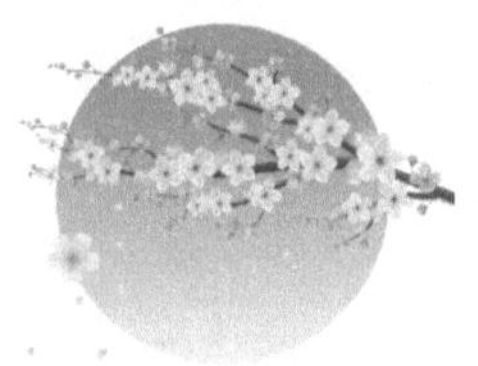

Chapter Eight

Dusk descended over Ship's Haven, the purple glow of twilight skies shimmering in the reflection of the sea. Reisu watched from the window of her office as the glow of the sun fully disappeared over the horizon. The bustle of the alley below her quieted as dockworkers and their families wandered into their homes. The silence of the street juxtaposed the din of music and chatter coming from the brothel's parlors, where the girls greeted their customers for the night. The faint click of the door opening behind her caught her attention.

"Maddox," she said with surprise on her face. "What are you doing back so soon?"

He strode across the room, leaning against the window frame beside her. "I found it," he said softly, his eyes focused on the alley below.

Reisu schooled her features, desperate to maintain composure. "You found it."

"You know where I'll be. Come find me when you have a moment to slip away."

She nodded, watching as Maddox twisted the shadows around himself and disappeared. With a sigh, she sat back down at her desk, the large ledger spread open before her, and picked up her pen to continue tallying the names of the guests who filtered past her open door toward the stairs.

Hours passed as she took notes and observed the flirtatious machinations of the girls as they manipulated their gentleman callers into any number of extra depravities on the menu for the evening. Finally, the flow of people ebbed to a slow trickle before stopping as the rooms upstairs were filled. Music still lingered in one of the parlors, where gentlemen sipped brandy as they awaited friends or their chosen companion's return. She took advantage of the lull, crossing to the large doors at the entrance of the room and closing them tightly, twisting the locks to hold them in place.

"At last," she whispered to herself as she moved toward the secret passageway tucked into the corner of the room. Her form shifted, shimmering wisps to pale flesh and back again, as she traversed the narrow stairs to Maddox's chambers. Knocking twice, she dragged her fingers along the wooden door toward the handle. "Maddox, open up."

He pulled the door open, gesturing her in. "Before I say anything... Kage is here."

"What?"

"Hi, Reisu," Kage said from the chair by the fire.

"Why is Kage here?" Reisu whispered to Maddox, narrowing her eyes.

"I think you'll find that Kage has more in common with us than you think," he said. "Let him explain, and we can decide what to do."

"Okay."

"Does that mean the Empress of Darkness will let me stay?" Kage asked.

"Empress of... Speak quickly before I shove my wisps down your throat until you choke on them," Reisu said.

Maddox rolled his eyes. "I found Kage in an...interesting position earlier," he said, wiggling his eyebrows and Reisu. "It seems my wayward little brother has been hiding at The Rusty Pig with the girl you saw."

"Her name is Sayah," Kage said. "And yes, I've been with her, helping her learn how to use her shadows to protect herself. Father has an interest in the girl."

"'An interest' is an understatement. He sent me hunting for her as soon as you failed to return," Maddox said. "Who is she, anyway?"

"Someone important," Kage said. "Father sent you and Dalton to kill her parents and take her years ago, but she hid before you could grab her."

The words brought a flicker of memory to the forefront of Reisu's mind. "The angel girl."

"That would explain a lot," Kage said. "She doesn't manipulate shadows so much as she twists the light around her, obscuring her in darkness."

Maddox looked thoughtful. "She was a little thing when I saw her last. We couldn't find her, and the bodies disappeared before I could return her mother to Dal'gon. Some lost love of his, I guess."

"No, someone he coveted," Reisu corrected him. "Though he courted her, she never accepted him. She was half angel, the daughter of one who gave up eternity for love. He wanted that power for himself, to breed a child that could eventually help him conquer the world. But that still doesn't tell me why you're here, Kage."

"I think Sayah can defeat him, Reisu."

She scoffed, rolling her eyes. "Try again."

"I mean it. The dagger, it can defeat him. He wants it, and he wants Sayah. I think that's because if she gets hold of the dagger, she can end him."

"With Dal'gon fixated on the dagger and the girl, we have a chance to put all the pieces into place to take him out. For good," Maddox said.

"Meet us at The Rusty Pig tonight," Kage said. "Once darkness has fallen, knock three times at the kitchen door. Bess will greet you there and take you up to our rooms."

"We will be there."

·‹‹•◆•››·

They sat together after Kage left, staring into the dying embers of the fire in the large stone fireplace.

"You said you found it," Reisu said, watching the burning logs pop and crash into the stone. "I thought you meant—"

"I did," Maddox interrupted. "I was able to shadow walk and locate your mother's diary amongst your family's belongings where they were moved after..."

"After they died without an heir. But you found it."

"It's on the table near the window."

She crossed the room and lifted the small book, its delicate leather binding beginning to crumble from age. "It's so much smaller than I remember it being," she said.

"Do you want to read it now, with me? Or would you prefer some privacy?" Maddox stroked one of his hands along her spine. "I can make myself scarce if you want to be alone while you read it."

"No," she whispered, leaning into his touch. "Stay with me."

He guided her to the bed, book in hand, and lay beside her, letting her curl against him as she flipped open the cover to reveal the delicate parchment within.

It is time. The cycle grows nearer, and Reisu has finally accepted her role in our family and this world.

Reisu chuckled. "Oh Mama, you never did stop hoping that I'd be a good little girl, did you?" she said under her breath before diving back into the diary.

Though she still chafes at the restrictions, especially those that keep her away from boys her age, she is already showing a great deal of promise. She is brave, strong, and wise well beyond her years. When she speaks, the other children listen to her without a thought, embracing her words as truth. Most impressive, perhaps, is the way she brings joy to others with just a smile or a kind word. Tsuki's kindness and persuasion are strong in her, and I suspect she will become even more powerful once she ascends.

I await further signs that Reisu is ready, but I fear that I may not be able to prepare her fully for the truth of her purpose. Without someone to guide her through the transition, I do not know what will become of my beloved girl...

Reisu wiped a tear from the corner of her eye and looked at Maddox. "What do you think this means?"

"That she loved you?" he asked. "And that she was trying to make sure you had the knowledge you needed to be able to ascend, as she calls it, when the time came."

"Ascend to become the Mistress of Night, whatever purpose that will serve." She sighed. "We still don't know what that entails, or if that could even happen now, after everything Dal'gon has forced me to do."

"Keep reading, maybe you'll learn more."

She nodded and flipped through the pages, passing over recountings of everyday occurrences that she'd long since forgotten. Her name jumped out at her from a page toward the middle of the book, drawing her attention.

A dark shadow has descended over our house. Rumors of an unknown man asking after Reisu reached us only yesterday, and I fear for what is coming. During our last offering to Tsuki, the flames glowed blue as Reisu approached, and a voice... A voice spoke to me.

"Fear the shadowed man. Only the shadows can steal the light of the moon from the Mistress of Night."

I've dreamed of it—of the shadowed man stealing Reisu away. She struggles with the increasing severity of our rules, but we can't allow her to be lost to the shadows. Without the Mistress of Night to ascend in her place, Tsuki will begin to fade and the world will be plunged into eternal darkness each night. So long as the Mistress of Night is safe and pure of heart, she will ascend and Tsuki won't fade.

Reisu looked at Maddox, watching as he read the last words on the page.

"I would assume," he said, "that you're still the Mistress of Night, Reisu."

She arched an eyebrow at him.

"The moon is still in the sky every night. So clearly Tsuki hasn't begun to fade."

Reisu sighed. "That doesn't mean she hasn't begun to fade. I've felt an emptiness on the nights when the moon darkens, like something vital has left me. I never stopped to wonder why... I've always assumed that feelings like that are because of the things I've done, the things Dal'gon has forced upon me. Maybe I'm feeling her fading because I'm not worthy to ascend."

"I don't think that's it," Maddox said. "If you weren't worthy, I don't think you'd sense anything."

"But what good is sensing it if I can't do anything about it?"

"Why do you think you can't do anything about it?"

"You know what he's done to me, Maddox," she said, her brow furrowed. "I am not pure of heart, I'm not safe. I haven't been safe a day since he stole me."

"But you're still alive, and unharmed, right? And you've carved out a niche for yourself here, a job where you protect others. You made yourself invaluable to Dal'gon, which kept you alive, even if it meant doing things that you wouldn't ever consider doing otherwise."

"I debased myself for him. Even though I despise him, even knowing that I want... I still did it. I ruined myself over and over again to protect myself, to preserve my worth as part of his twisted little family."

"You did what you had to do to stay alive, Reisu. There is no shame in protecting yourself. It doesn't lessen your worth to keep yourself safe." Maddox pulled her closer, pillowing her head on his shoulder. He pressed a kiss to her forehead. "Your value wasn't lost because you had to make tough choices. You are stronger because of it."

She snuggled closer to him, closing her eyes and letting him bring her comfort. "I don't know where to begin," she admitted. "I stopped believing I was still worthy so many years ago."

"You were always worthy, Reisu. You must believe that your worth is not tied to what was stripped from you, but to what you have made of yourself as a result."

She hummed thoughtfully and nuzzled her nose against his neck. "Show me my worth," she whispered.

He tilted her chin toward him, kissing her deeply. "As you wish."

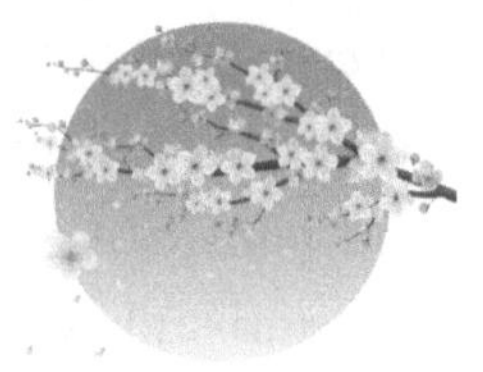

Chapter Nine

Maddox trailed after Reisu as they headed toward The Rusty Pig to meet Kage and Sayah to go over the plan one more time. The cramped alleys of the dock district surrounded them, hiding them from passersby on the main streets leading down to the port.

"This way," Maddox said, lunging forward to grasp Reisu's wrist and yank her to the side.

"What the hell, Maddox? I'm more than capable of—" Her voice cut off as he slammed a hand over her mouth and pinned her into the wall.

"Keep your damn mouth closed for a moment," he whispered. "Someone is coming, and I can feel the shadows reacting to whoever it is." He wrapped shadows around them, blending them into the stacks of boxes and crates that filled the alley as he kept watch.

Reisu held herself stiff against him, her eyes wide as she watched the shadows undulate in the alley. Maddox's hand remained over her mouth, reminding her to keep quiet and still as his eyes searched the area around them for the intruder. The sound of humming, barely audible, approached them. At the sound, Maddox relaxed slightly, shifting his hand away from Reisu's mouth, his eyes twinkling.

"Gods dammit, Kage," he said, releasing the shadows from around them. "You scared the shit out of us."

"Apologies, brother. When I told Sayah of our plan and your agreement that action must be taken, she admitted still fears you. After the little stunt you pulled the last time you saw her, I couldn't help but understand her concern, so I figured I would escort you," Kage said, sketching a bow. "Follow me."

The trio walked through the alley and knocked three times on the kitchen door. A curvy redhead swung the top half of the door open and peered down at them.

"Kage," she said in a voice like rich honey. "This them?"

"Sure is. Reisu, Maddox, this is Bess. The best cook in Ship's Haven, by far," Kage said, gesturing to Reisu and Maddox in turn.

The corners of Bess's full lips tilted up. "Hurt my girl and I will end you all, shadow powers or not," she said.

"Sayah's in the rooms upstairs. Kage can show you the way."

They passed through the door and up the stairs, entering a well-appointed set of rooms. A tea service was spread across a table at the center of the sitting room, a tiered tray of treats surrounded by a glorious array of sandwiches and several pots of tea. Sayah launched herself from a chair beside the fire, landing in Kage's arms and kissing him soundly.

"Sayah, this is my brother, Maddox, and Reisu, our—

"Wraith," Reisu said softly. "Dal'gon once hunted me much the way he has been hunting you."

Kage's eyes widened. "I didn't know..."

"It's ok, it was many years before your birth. We no longer discuss it, since he's moved on to other...fixations."

Sayah stared at Reisu, confused. "What is a wraith?"

Reisu willed her form back to wisps, shifting into the smoke lingering above the candles at the center of the table, then moving back to corporeal form beside Maddox. Sayah gaped at her, unsure what to think.

"I was made into a spy, an assassin, to carry out Dal'gon's will in an effort to keep me from fulfilling a prophecy that was revealed at my birth. They named me the Mistress of Night, heir apparent to Tsuki, the Lunar Goddess of my people." Reisu paused, reaching out to grasp Sayah's hand. "This is a lot to take in. Why don't we sit and eat some of this lovely spread while I tell you my story? I have a weakness for clotted cream on my scones."

Sayah nodded, and the group seated themselves around the table. Smiling, Reisu spread clotted cream onto a cinnamon scone.

"Oh gods, this is exceptional," she mumbled around the delicate crumb of the scone in her mouth.

"I told you, best cook in Ship's Haven," Kage said with a smirk.

"I hate to admit that you're right, but you are. This time," Maddox said, leaning back in his chair and wiping a bit of cucumber sandwich from his lips. "She even makes cucumber sandwiches delicious."

"It's the poppy seeds and roasted garlic," Sayah said. "They're my favorite."

Reisu sighed, leaning back in her chair and patting her stomach lightly. "Whatever it is, it's certainly better than what Dal'gon's chef whips up. I could live here forever."

Maddox smiled, his eyes alight as he witnessed the pleasure on Reisu's face. "Maybe we can convince Bess to come work for us once we get rid of him."

Sayah jumped, her eyes wide. "Once we what?"

Reisu looked at Maddox from the corner of her eye. "What did she think we were doing here?" she asked under her breath.

"That's what I was telling you, love," Kage said, reaching across the table to grasp her hand. "They're fighting against him, too."

"But why? He," she said, gesturing at Maddox with her free hand, "attacked us not even a week ago. This doesn't make sense."

"I know it doesn't seem realistic," Reisu said. "I know it's hard to trust us. But I have every reason to want Dal'gon out of the picture. Not only for what he did to me. What he continues to do to me. What he took—"

"From both of us, Reisu. What he took from both of us." Maddox looked at Sayah. "As long as he lives, Reisu and I can never truly be together."

"Why?"

"Reisu belongs to Dal'gon," Kage said. "Father doesn't allow anyone else to touch his toys."

Reisu flinched.

"Sorry, Rei. I couldn't think of a better way to say it."

"It's unfortunate, but accurate," she said. "As I was saying, I have my own reasons for wanting him gone."

"To be clear," Maddox said, "Reisu and I are here to help you and Kage with whatever harebrained scheme my little brother has come up with. Dal'gon has grown too comfortable in his power, and he will stop at nothing until he obtains you, Sayah."

"You can think what you want of us, and I know you've heard less-than-savory things about us. But I will not let him ruin another young woman's life the way he ruined mine." Reisu locked eyes with Sayah. "Or worse, the way he ruined Kage's mother's life. Used as a brood mare until she was nothing but a shell of a woman."

Sayah shuddered. "Kage, you didn't tell me—"

"I didn't want to scare you, love." He gripped her hand tighter.

Reisu looked at them, a small smile on her face. "I think I have an idea of how we can defeat him. We'll need to get the dagger that Kage retrieved out of the safe in Dal'gon's study..."

The tension was nearly unbearable.

"Listen, Reisu. I don't want to tell you what to do," Maddox said as they walked back into the alley behind The Rusty Pig. "But if you don't reach out and take what you want, what are you even living for?"

"Take what I want?" Reisu asked. "What are you talking about?"

"You just go through life maintaining the *status quo*, never taking chances, never going after what you want. If you—"

Reisu cut him off. "You know me so well, right? If you know me so well, tell me what I want," she taunted, appalled by Maddox's bullheaded determination that he knew best for her, regardless of her desires.

"Me. You want me, even though you refuse to admit it to yourself," he said, a smirk on his

face.

She stared at him, shock on her face.

"And, even more than that, you're scared of how much you want me," he said. "You're scared because you don't want to have these big emotions for anyone, you promised yourself it would never happen again, and here you are. Wanting. Desiring. Loving."

"I don't—" she trailed off, pursing her lips.

"You can't even deny it, can you? You love me, and it's got you so tied up inside that you don't know which way is up anymore."

She shook her head. "Is this about me not responding and agreeing when you mentioned Dal'gon was keeping us apart earlier? I don't understand where all of this," she said, waving her hand at the space between them, "is coming from."

"Tell me you feel nothing when I do this," Maddox challenged before claiming her lips with his own. He nipped at her lower lip with his teeth before sliding his tongue into the soft chasm of her mouth.

Her body swayed into his, her arms wrapping around his neck of their own volition. Hearts beating in time, he pressed his body into hers, marveling at the fit of their every dip and curve. He broke the kiss after several long moments, smiling at the dazed look in her eyes as they stared at one another.

"Tell me you felt nothing," he said again.

"I can't. Because I do. No matter how hard I try, no matter how much I tell myself that this means nothing to me... I do. I feel something for you."

"You love me, Reisu. Say it." He growled low in his throat, frustration etched across his rugged features. "Fuck it, I'll say it first. I love you," he said, wrapping her in his arms again. "I love you."

"You'll be the death of me, you know," she said, grazing his shoulder with her teeth. "I love you, too."

He growled, pushing their bodies into the rough stone wall of the tavern. He slid his hand up her leg, pushing up her skirts to find the delicate skin of her thigh. A feral smile twisted his lips as she gasped, pressing her body closer to his fingertips. Reisu reached for the laces at the waist of his breeches, pulling them loose and freeing his length.

"Mmm," she moaned against his lips. She gripped his cock, stroking her thumb across the sensitive tip. Pulling back from his kiss, she locked eyes with him as she wiped the bead of moisture from his tip and then slowly licked the remnants of it from her fingers.

Maddox's pupils dilated as he watched her tongue lap at her fingertips. He gripped her thighs, positioning himself against the slick folds of her core, and thrust forward, seating himself to the hilt inside her tight heat as he captured her lips with his to trap her moan. Shadows undulated from his skin, twisting to hide them from any passersby as they moved together.

Reisu grasped at his shoulders, his hair, the old stones of the building, grappling for purchase as pleasure built within her. He ran his fingers through her hair, letting the silken texture flow across his skin before sliding his hand down her neck and across the smooth skin between her breasts. She writhed against him as he rolled her nipple between his fingers before dragging his hand down her abdomen to circle the sensitive bundle of nerves between her legs. Her teeth dug into her lower lip as he stroked her in time with his thrusts—her back bowed, her skin aflame as the orgasm ripped through her. Her wisps danced free, flickering amongst Maddox's shadows as he tumbled over the edge alongside her.

He rested his head against her shoulder, his body pressing hers into the rough stone of the wall. A sigh slipped from her throat, and she pressed a kiss to his temple.

"Say it again," he whispered.

"I love you."

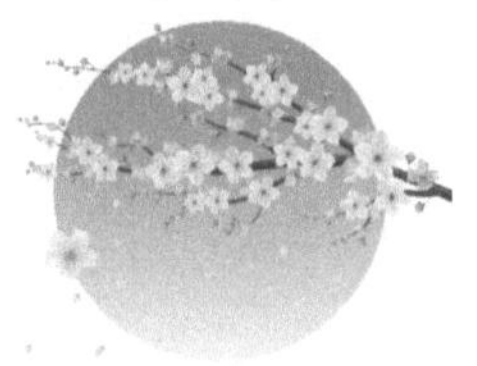

Chapter Ten

The sun rose, painting the sky in pastels over the harbor like every other morning. Maddox and Reisu stood side by side in the window of her office, watching in silence as dawn broke across Ship's Haven. She leaned her head against his shoulder, pulling his arm around her. Mist rose from the cobblestone street, reminding her of the way her wisps shimmered in the sunlight.

"You think this is what we're meant to do?" she asked, angling her head to look up at Maddox.

"I think we have to take the risk, or we'll be trapped here forever."

"What if he catches me while I'm retrieving the dagger?"

"He won't, we'll keep him distracted." Maddox cupped her cheek. "You will be safe, and then we'll be free."

Reisu nodded.

"Everything is going to be ok."

"I know," she whispered. "I'm just afraid it won't be the same."

‹‹•●•››

The study door was closed when Reisu approached, her wisps shifting in and out of the shadows in the hallway. She hovered just outside the door, listening for movement inside before sliding beneath the door like smoke. She pushed herself into the corner near the fireplace, hidden in the shadows and smoke from the crackling flames.

Okay, she thought. *Grab the key, get the dagger, then into the passageway and back to my chambers.* She sprang into action, moving quietly as she sneaked the key from its hiding spot and pulled the books to free the facade covering the safe. Once the dagger was in hand and the safe was re-secured, she slipped into the passageway and hurried toward her own chambers two levels down.

After locking her door, she threw herself into the deep cushioned chair beside the fireplace and removed the dagger from its hiding place in her skirts. The light of the fire threw part of the engraving into shadow. A small discrepancy in the symbols caught her eye; she tilted the dagger's hilt backward, watching as the moon closest to the quillon shifted from a waxing crescent moon to a full moon and back with her movements. She stroked her fingertip across the moon, a sharp gasp leaving her as the skin ripped open. Blood filled the carved moon, the engraved night sky beginning to glow as it spread through the whorls and swirls.

Reisu watched in awe as light rippled through the dagger; pressure built inside her, something shifting as the dagger glowed brighter and brighter. Her skin heated, a burning sensation in her hands forcing her to drop the dagger, sending it crashing to the ground. She sprang to her feet, her head swimming as a ripple of fear rushed through her.

"What—" she startled, her breath caught in her throat as she caught a glimpse of herself in the mirror. Her skin shimmered, a delicate glow dancing across her features. "What is happening?"

The quiet voice from her memories whispered to her again. "Reisu Heiwa, you are ascending."

"Who... what?"

"You are the Mistress of Night, Reisu. Chosen by me at birth to be the one to ascend and rule the night in my place during my eternal rest. You have been reunited with the moon dagger; your blood has awakened the blade and begun the ascension," Tsuki said as she appeared to Reisu in the mirror. Her straight black hair hung to her hips, shining in Reisu's glow. "I'm sure you have many questions, my child, but we have limited time. We must—"

"How can I ascend?" Reisu interrupted. "I am no longer pure. Dal'gon saw to that."

"Purity of heart is not something that can be erased, Reisu. The shadow demon's attempts to sully you did not change who you are at your core. I saw this in you so many years ago—the desire to help others, to protect those you love, the need to experience life fully." Tsuki paused. "You have believed, for all these years, that you were no longer worthy because of what was done to you. But when you were given the chance to take back your autonomy, to protect an innocent from the fate that awaited her, you took it. You have always been worthy, Reisu. Dal'gon's actions did not strip that from you. You only had to rediscover your worth to be able to start your ascent."

Reisu stared at Tsuki in the mirror. "My mother always said you were our patron Goddess, that you had taken special interest in me."

"She was correct. Your mother was my most devoted acolyte, and her love for me never wavered, even after your disappearance. I brought her comfort many nights, showing her glimpses of you, letting her know you were alive and safe."

"She knew. But the histories—"

"We hid it from the rest of the world. To everyone, you were lost, presumed to have drowned in the lake. But she knew. And now, my child, you must complete your tasks before the ascension is complete."

"But what do I do, how do I tell—"

"You will be able to tell him. He will understand."

"What do I need to do?"

"Put the dagger in place and help the girl dismantle the shadow demon's hold."

Reisu nodded. She felt the ghost of a touch on her shoulder, watching in the mirror as Tsuki removed her hand, beginning to fade.

"You will complete your ascension before dawn, my child. The pieces are in place, and you have everything you need. Be well."

Tsuki disappeared from the mirror, leaving Reisu alone, staring at her reflection. "I was always worthy," she whispered, studying herself with new clarity. "I was always worthy."

"I mean, I've been telling you that," Maddox said as the door to the hidden passageway swung open. "There was never anything wrong with you. My father, on the other hand..."

"How much did you hear?" Reisu asked as she turned to him.

"Just what you said as I walked in." He wrapped his arms around her, dropping a kiss onto her forehead. "You're glowing."

"I've begun to ascend," she admitted. "The dagger, it was the key all along."

"The key to your ascension? Or to ending Dal'gon?"

"According to Tsuki... Both."

"You had a conversation with a Goddess?" Maddox looked flummoxed.

"Yes," Reisu said quietly. "When I was studying the dagger, the engraving sliced my fingertip open. My blood inside the dagger began the ascension and allowed her to visit me for a moment. We have to get the dagger into place for Sayah and ensure everything moves forward as planned."

He nodded, lifting the dagger from the floor. "I'll get this to Kage. Do whatever you need to do."

"Maddox," she said, grabbing his wrist. "I don't know what ascending will do to me or what will happen once it is complete. Please know—"

"I know," he said. He pulled her to him, pressing his lips to hers. "I love you." He handed her the dagger.

"I have to meet Kage in Dal'gon's study, then help prepare Dal'gon for the girl. Will you join me once it's over?" she asked.

"Of course."

Once everything was in place and her part had been played, Reisu sneaked back into her room and undressed, wrapping herself in her favorite dressing gown. Minutes slipped into hours as she sat beside her fire, feeling the pressure of the tides pulling and pushing against her. Her glow dimmed, matching the waning crescent moon in the sky. The brothel fell silent as its doors swung closed behind the last patron. The air felt heavy, full of building tension, and shuffling feet in the corridor beyond her chambers drew her attention to her door as it swung open.

"Reisu," Maddox said, crossing the room toward her. "It is done."

She nodded, feeling the bubble of tension burst. It sent a tremble through the building, seeming to shake the very foundation. As though on cue, the tides seemed to raise, the sound of water crashing against the shore reaching them through her open windows. The first rays of light appeared on the horizon, dimming Reisu's glow further as the moon's light disappeared into the growing light of day. Maddox grasped her hand, urging her to stand, and they watched the sunrise as a new day broke over Ship's Haven.

"Do you feel any different?" he asked.

"I can feel everything. The turning of the earth, the changing of the tides, the gentle glow of the sun against the moon's surface. But I'm still here."

"I'm glad," he said. "It would be pretty difficult for me to ask you to marry me if you left."

A gasp caught in Reisu's throat as she whipped around to face him. "What?"

"It's done," Maddox said again. "Dal'gon is defeated. Gone. We are all free."

"Free," she whispered, leaning her forehead against his broad chest.

"Free at last."

Reisu pushed up on the tips of her toes, closing the distance between them and pressing her lips to his. "Yes," she said.

"Say it again."

She giggled as he pulled her toward the bed. "I love you."

Acknowledgements

Being an author would be exceptionally difficult without the incredible people I've surrounded myself with.

To my amazing editor, Lisa Morris – thank you for putting up with my imposter syndrome, shenanigans, and semantic debates. I am so lucky to have found you.

To my husband, Mick – this novella was hard to write, and even harder to finish because of graduate school, editing schedules, a day job, and our wonderful children. Thank you for always supporting me, filling my water bottle, and making sure I eat so that I don't get hangry. You're the best partner and friend ever, and I'm so grateful for you every day. Je t'aime!

To my children, who have taught me resilience and patience – thank you for putting up with me (and for not being too embarrassed when your friends ask for copies of my books). Love you all to the moon and back.

To Aunt Cindy – thank you for being my biggest fan and for always commenting on my posts on Facebook. You make me smile every day. Love you!

To Cassandra L. Thompson and the coolest Crows I've ever known – thank you all for being the most amazing friends a girl could ask for.

About the author

Tiffany Putenis holds a Masters degree in English and Creative Writing from Southern New Hampshire University. Her love for the written word started at an early age, and she continues to be fascinated by works of fiction. She counts Robert Jordan, Brandon Sanderson, Amber V. Nicole, and Nisha J. Tuli among the authors who revived her love of fantasy and romantasy stories. Though her favorite stories in recent years have been fantasy, she still has a healthy love of vampires that started in high school when she discovered Bram Stoker and Anne Rice. She works as an editor for Quill and Crow Publishing House in addition to writing her own works of fiction.

Tiffany lives in the American Northeast with her husband, three kids, one dog, and two cats. She finds solace in hiking through the beautiful forests that surround her home. You can find Tiffany on TikTok (@tputeniswrites) and Instagram/Threads (@TPutenisWrites). You can also visit her website at www.tiffanyputenis.com for updates.

Also By Tiffany Putenis

Ship's Haven Stories:
Daughter of Shadows

Standalone Novels:
Into the Shadowlands

Anthologies featuring Tiffany Putenis
Of Cottages and Cauldrons
Of Mistletoe and Snow
Haunted: A Crow Anthology
Renascentem: Crow Calls Volume VI